Granny's Giant Bannock

By Brenda Isabel Wastasecoot
Illustrated by Kimberly McKay-Fleming

PEMMICAN
PUBLICATIONS
INC.

Pemmican Publications gratefully acknowledges the assistance accorded to its publishing program by the Manitoba Arts Council, the Province of Manitoba – Department of Culture, Heritage and Tourism, Canada Council for the Arts and Canadian Heritage – Book Publishing Industry Development Program.

Printed and Bound in Canada.
First printing: 2008   Second printing 2010   Third printing 2013

Library and Archives Canada Cataloguing in Publication

Wastasecoot, Brenda Isabel, 1963-
    Granny's giant bannock / written by Brenda Isabel Wastasecoot ; illustrated by Kimberly McKay-Fleming.

ISBN 978-1-894717-49-6

    1. Métis–Juvenile fiction. I. McKay-Fleming, Kimberly, 1968- II. Title.

PS8645.A833G73 2008   jC813'.6   C2008-905865-8

**PEMMICAN
PUBLICATIONS
INC.**
Committed to the promotion of Metis culture and heritage

90 Sutherland Ave., Winnipeg, Manitoba,
R2W 3C7 Canada
www.pemmicanpublications.ca

  Canadian Heritage Patrimoine canadien  Canada Council for the Arts Conseil des Arts du Canada  MANITOBA ARTS COUNCIL CONSEIL DES ARTS DU MANITOBA YEARS/ANS   Manitoba

I dedicate this book to my mother, Maria Wastasecoot, who let me bake my bannock in peanut butter jar lids.

Being a mom offers many opportunities to be creative, and this was one way to make bedtime a fun time with much affection and laughter too. Where adults get so bogged down with the realities of life, children are able to simply enjoy their ability to imagine. This story grew out of having to make up stories for my daughter Dayle. I would try to hold her attention long enough for her to settle down to sleep, and depending on how she would respond to the story I would have to make it more or less believable. She would also add to the story, and so over the years it has grown to be not just a bannock story but also a Giant Bannock story.

When I was growing up in a large Cree family as the youngest of 10 children, bannock was an important supplement to our soups and stews of caribou, moose and fish. It was also a favourite snack and could be easily whipped up for visitors and their children. Some of my happiest memories of growing up are the smell of mother's freshly baked bannock and lots of cousins to share it with. The making of bannock is a skill that can be perfected with many years of practice.

Larf went to meet his granny at the bus depot. She was down for a visit all the way from the beautiful northern town of Thompson, where she and most of their family lived. Larf lived in the small city of Brandon, where he attended university to become a teacher. His granny wanted to keep him company for a while and to see the sights of Brandon.

"Noosisim," she said with a big smile as she climbed down the steps of the Grey Goose bus.

"Tansi, kookoom," Larf replied as he helped his granny down the last step onto the city pavement of Brandon.

"Wachay," she said as she gave him a big grandmother hug.

It was an exciting day for them both. Granny had never been to a city before and she was eager to see what it had to offer. She wanted to see all of the fabric stores to buy cloth for her star quilt project, and the craft stores to see what colours of beads they had for moccasins.

Granny would have to rely on Larf to take her to these stores and to speak English for her. She only spoke Cree and understood very little in English. Larf was only able to understand some of her Cree words. They communicated with some Cree words and some English words. They used hand signs and pictures of things or facial expressions to communicate. Most of the time everything worked out OK. This is a story of one of those times.

Granny loved to cook and make bannock for her grandchildren. One day Larf asked Granny to make some bannock. He knew how to say some words in their language, and this was one phrase he had to learn if he wanted to have the best bannock in the world.

"Granny, bannock-ihkew anoost?" He asked Granny if she would make some bannock today.

Granny knew what Larf wanted. She looked in his cupboards to see if he had all the ingredients to make bannock. She noticed one special ingredient was missing. He didn't have any baking powder, which is a very important ingredient to make the bannock soft and fluffy. She told him in Cree what he needed to buy at the grocery store. She tried to tell him he needed some Machik Baking Powder.

"Mumatawisewin, machik." Granny tried to emphasize her words, and drew a picture in the air of a big bannock. She described the bannock rising big and fluffy, and then she added another Cree phrase, "ta misak" (so it will get very big).

Larf nodded with a smile, agreeing to run to the store before his class. He thought he might have just enough time to go there and back before his very first class that week.

At the grocery store there were many kinds of ingredients for baking. He didn't know there could be so many baking ingredients just for bannock. His eyes scanned the long row of products on the shelf. Which one did Granny want? He tried to remember, but was now in a hurry to get to his class. Can you remember what kind of baking powder Granny wanted? One brightly coloured jar caught his eye. It said: SHAZZAM! He quickly read the label to make sure it would be good enough for Granny's bannock. He smiled to himself, thinking, "This is exactly what we need for a yummy bannock."

He returned home with a bright red jar with a label that read: Super-duper-fastest-acting-highest-concentrated-solar-powered-shazzam-yeast.

Granny looked at the jar, and she didn't recognize it at all. She asked him if he was sure this was the powder she needed, because it looked different from the kind she bought all the time at home in Thompson. Not understanding all her words, and too rushed to see what was wrong, Larf encouraged his granny to try this new powder for now. He had to leave in a hurry to get to his class. He did not want to be late. He did not have time now to run back to the store. He would have to take Granny there later if she wanted to go get a different ingredient for her bannock.

"Bye Kookoom!" Larf called to her as he ran out the door.

Now it was only Granny and Sam the cat left to decide what to do. *Do you think Granny should use the SHAZZAM powder that Larf bought from the store? Do you think she will try to make the bannock with it?*

Granny couldn't read the words of warning on the label:

CAUTION: apply only ¼ teaspoon per 10 cups of flour. She trusted her grandson, and so she used five heaping tablespoons, like she usually did when she used her regular baking powder.

On that beautiful sunny afternoon, after mixing all the ingredients together in a large silver bowl, Granny left the dough to rise while she watched her favourite game show on TV. She fell asleep for what seemed like only minutes. While she was sleeping in front of the TV, the bannock rose so high it began flowing over the rim of the big silver bowl. Sam, the cat, watched cautiously with much curiosity and was careful to keep a safe distance from the growing bannock. His sensitive ears could hear the dough filling with air as it grew outward and upward. He watched it fall to the floor and slowly spread itself out, reaching higher and higher as it grew.

When Granny awoke she remembered her bannock. She went to the kitchen to check on it and to get it ready for the oven. *Can you guess how big the bannock got?*

By the time Granny went to check on her bannock it had risen to enormous heights. It filled the whole kitchen! Sam the cat was nowhere to be seen. And Granny could not even enter the kitchen, because the doorway was blocked by the bannock dough. What could she do?

She decided to attack the bannock and try to punch it down to a more manageable size. Granny punched and wrestled with the bannock, but she was no match. Granny fell into the bannock!

The bannock had Granny and it was still growing. It began to roll down the hallway toward the screen door. The bannock popped the screen door off its hinges and was leaving the house! The postal carrier was just about to put some letters into the mailbox when the bannock gobbled her up too!

Larf had just come around the corner from the University to see the ever-growing and rising bannock roll down the front steps and onto the sidewalk. Just then, a boy on his red bicycle came riding by and – OOPS! – the big bannock gobbled up the boy and his red bicycle! A man on a noisy motorcycle was zooming down Thirteenth Street. Do you think he escaped the rolling ball of dough? NO! The Giant Bannock rolled right over him too, and then the street was quiet again.

Larf ran into the house to find Granny. "Kookoom!"

He called and looked around the house, but she was not there.

His eyes grew very big when he realized that the Giant Bannock might have taken his grandmother too. He phoned the police.

"Slow down son, I can hardly hear what you're telling me. It's a giant…what?" An officer on the other end of the phone was speaking very slowly.

It was too slowly for Larf. "A Giant Bannock swallowed a boy on a bicycle, and I think it took my granny too!" He knew how unbelievable he sounded, but he hoped the officer at the other end of phone would be able to help him.

"OK, young man, I am not in the mood for pranks. Wait a minute, I have to put you on hold…"

Larf dropped the phone and ran out the door, shouting for his grandmother as he frantically followed the slowly rolling, rising ball of dough.

The next sound he heard was the sirens of the police cars coming closer and closer. Other witnesses had also called in, and now the whole fleet of police cars with all their lights flashing surrounded the Giant Bannock that was growing rapidly. It was now as big as the church on the corner. Some of the police cars were racing ahead of the Giant Bannock as the police rushed to stop people and cars from getting trapped.

It was the wind from the northwest that was moving the Giant Bannock south on Thirteenth Street toward a very busy street, Victoria Avenue, where lots of cars and trucks and semi-trailers intersected. As the wind shifted more toward the east, the slowly rolling Giant Bannock changed direction too!

Which way will it go next?

It moved east toward the grocery stores, where everyone in town did their shopping. It was a bright warm day to be out walking, and it seemed like everyone decided to do their shopping that day. There were people walking their dogs, people pushing babies in strollers and there were even people on roller blades. People had no idea what they were about to see rolling toward them.

Victoria Avenue was swarming as the police scurried to block the side streets to stop the Giant Bannock from taking another surprise turn! Following the police cars was the big red fire engine with a louder siren and more lights flashing. Would the wind change direction and stop the Bannock from rolling into the grocery stores? No one knew where the Giant Bannock would roll next. No one knew how big the Giant Bannock would get.

What will they do to protect the people from the Giant Bannock? What would you do?

A brave firefighter jumped off the fire engine to save a mom pushing her baby in a stroller who was about to cross Victoria Avenue. Some people ran out of the way as they saw the Giant Bannock approaching. But mostly people just moved out of the way and watched with awe and disbelief. Where did this giant ball of dough come from? How did it get so big? And who was responsible for such a marvelous magical sight?

The Giant Bannock rolled into the parking lot, where it hit the grocery store. It was so big it blocked the doorways. No one could get into the store and no one could get out. There it stopped rolling and there it stopped growing. It was now still and quiet, but it was as big as the supermarket! Everyone gathered around. They stopped in their cars and walked toward the Giant Bannock. Dogs stopped in their tracks and looked up too. Cats in apartment windows were captivated by all the excitement.

By now Larf had caught up with the police cars and fire engine and alerted them to his granny being stuck in the Giant Bannock. "There may be others trapped in there!" he shouted.

The wind had softened to a warm breeze, and in the hot sun something was happening to the Giant Bannock. What do you think the Giant Bannock did next? What happens to dough when it gets hot? It starts to bake. The Giant Bannock now rested, and it covered the whole parking lot with Granny, a postal carrier, the little boy on his red bicycle and also the man on a motorcycle still stuck inside it.

The firefighters used their tools and carefully carved a hole into the freshly baked, soft and fluffy bannock. Everyone watched as the firefighters tried to get through the Giant Bannock dough. After what seemed like only seconds, amazingly, the man on his motorcycle emerged from the Giant Bannock. Next came the little boy on his red bicycle, and then came the postal carrier with her bag of letters. But where was Granny?

"Granny must be in there!" Larf called out to the firefighters.

And seconds later Granny appeared. She was holding Sam the cat, too!

"Noosisim!" she called out to her grandson.

Granny gave Larf a big, grandmother hug, with Sam the cat between them.

Larf was very happy to see that his grandmother and his cat were safe.

Everyone in the parking lot clapped and cheered. They couldn't help but notice the smell of this freshly baked Giant Bannock. What better way to celebrate than to have some! All the firemen helped Granny and Larf share the most delicious bannock in the world.

When shoppers came out of the store through the long tunnel cut out by the firefighters, Granny invited them to have some with the rest of the crowd. They came out with butter and jam to have with the bannock. It was yummy!

Everyone in town came to see the Giant Bannock. With a bannock that big, people from miles away could smell it baking. They followed their noses to find it. They brought their tea and lawn chairs and joined the feast! People of different colours and different languages sat together and ate. It tasted delicious to everyone, no matter what language they spoke. Even the police officers and firefighters sat and enjoyed some bannock and tea.

People came to ask Granny and Larf what happened to their bannock. "How did it get so big?" they asked. Only Sam the Cat really knew what happened, and he was not telling anyone.

Larf told his Granny how happy he was that she was safe. Granny nodded, but didn't really know what Larf was saying. She told him in her Cree words that he bought the wrong ingredient for her bannock, but Larf didn't really understand her either.

What do you think Larf should do next time? What could Granny do to help him?

Bannock Recipe

6 cups (1.5 L) of flour

3 tablespoons (45 mL) of baking powder (not yeast)

1 tablespoon (15 mL) of salt

1 cup (250 mL) of lard

3 to 4 cups (750 mL to 1 L) of warm water

Preheat the oven to about 350 F (170 C)

In a very big bowl, pour 6 cups of flour. Mix flour, baking powder and salt together. Make a hole in the middle and put in 1 cup of lard (slightly softened). With your hands, mix flour and lard together until the flour mixture absorbs most of the lard. Add the water gradually, and work it into a dough so it is no longer sticky but also not too dry. Spread the dough out on a large cookie sheet; poke holes in it with a fork. Bake at 350 F for about 20 minutes or until golden brown, turning it over halfway.

Glossary

Bannock-ihkew	make bannock
Anoosht	today
Kookoom	grandmother
Machik	Cree pronunciation of the word "magic"
Mumatawisewin	magic
Noosisim	grandson
Tansi	How are you?
Wachay	greetings